THE PRINCESS WHO HAD

Almost EVERYTHING

Mireille Levert   Josée Masse

Tundra Books

Published in Canada by Tundra Books,
75 Sherbourne Street, Toronto, Ontario M5A 2P9

Published in the United States by Tundra Books of Northern New York,
P.O. Box 1030, Plattsburgh, New York 12901

Library of Congress Control Number: 2008900478

Library and Archives Canada Cataloguing in Publication

Levert, Mireille

[Princesse qui avait presque tout. English]

   The princess who had almost everything / Mireille Levert ; illustrations by Josée Masse.

Translation of: La princesse qui avait presque tout.

ISBN 978-0-88776-887-3

I. Masse, Josée II. Title. III. Title : Princesse qui avait presque tout. English.

PS8573.E956355P7413 2008   jC843'.54   C2008-900384-5

We acknowledge the financial support of the Government of Canada through the Book Publishing Industry Development Program and that of the Government of Ontario through the Ontario Media Development Corporation's Ontario Book Initiative. We further acknowledge the support of the Canada Council for the Arts and the Ontario Arts Council for our publishing program.

ONTARIO ARTS COUNCIL
CONSEIL DES ARTS DE L'ONTARIO

Design by Leah Springate

Printed in China

1 2 3 4 5 6   13 12 11 10 09 08

To Jacob Lanny, my first professor
of fine arts – ML

To Mireille, to whom I said,
"I am overjoyed, thanks to
your words" – JM

Along time ago, if you looked
very far off into the distance, you would see a hill. And at the
very top of that hill you would see a castle, as lovely a castle as
there ever was. And if you looked harder yet, you would see
Alicia, the princess who lived in the castle. Her parents loved
her dearly and did everything they could to make her happy.
But every day and every night, no matter how far away
you stood, you would always hear Alicia yell,
"I'M BORED!"

The king and queen thought and thought about ways to amuse Alicia. A famous architect built a magnificent castle for the princess, and the people of the kingdom gathered to see him unveil it. It was the finest castle ever seen, they all agreed, what with its turrets and its own built-in roller coaster. They clapped their hands and cheered. Not Alicia. "It's horrible," was all she had to say.

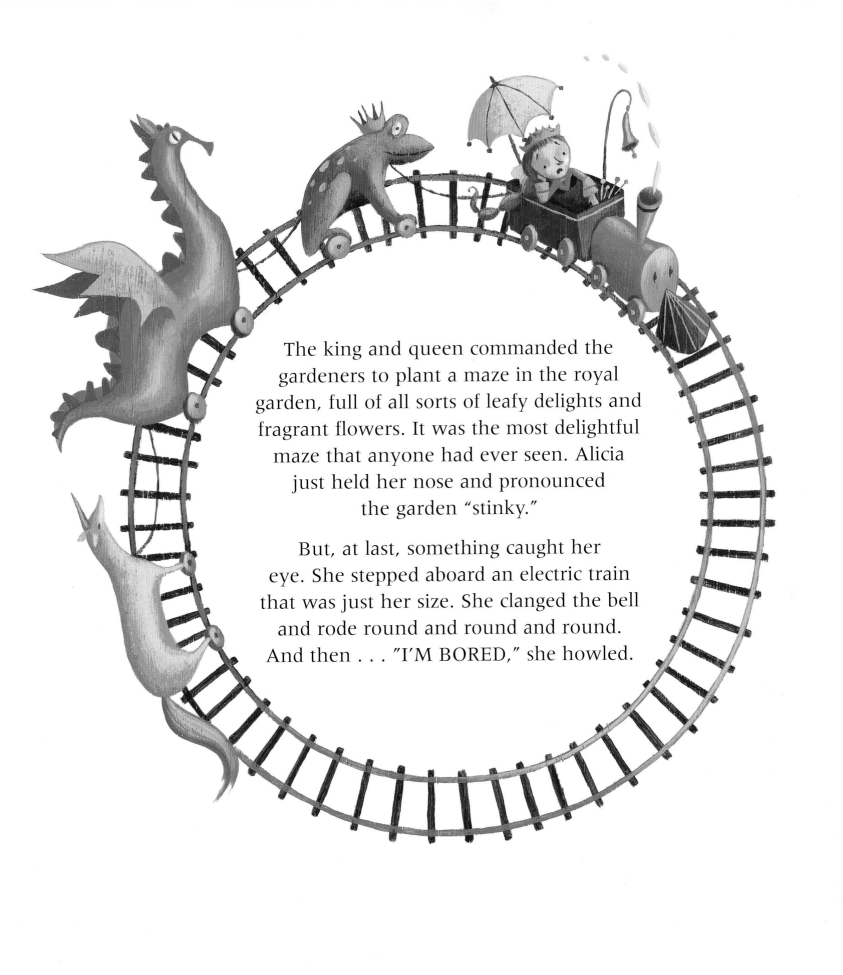

The king and queen commanded the gardeners to plant a maze in the royal garden, full of all sorts of leafy delights and fragrant flowers. It was the most delightful maze that anyone had ever seen. Alicia just held her nose and pronounced the garden "stinky."

But, at last, something caught her eye. She stepped aboard an electric train that was just her size. She clanged the bell and rode round and round and round. And then . . . "I'M BORED," she howled.

Alicia got off the train. She tried to take a step, but she felt as if the ground was rolling under her feet. "I'm dizzy! I can't walk straight," she shouted. She was still shouting when her servants arrived to carry her back to the castle.

The shoemaker was waiting with the finest wares to tempt her. They didn't. She tried on a delicate pair of golden slippers, perfect for dancing. "Do I look like a miniature princess? These are too small." She frowned.

Next, she tried on sturdy boots, perfect for climbing up and down the castle hill. "Do you think I'm an elephant?" She grimaced.

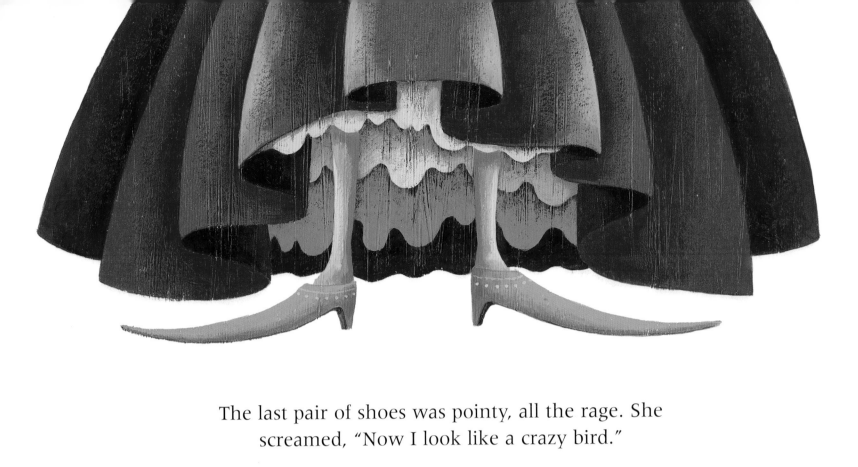

The last pair of shoes was pointy, all the rage. She screamed, "Now I look like a crazy bird."

If the shoemaker wanted to answer, we will never know because he was drowned out by a fantastic, rafter-shaking bellow.
"I'M BORED!"

Alicia kicked off her pointy shoes and ran barefoot across the court to the dining room. The royal bakers had created a dessert wonderland: mountains of cakes, shimmering jellies, and lavish cupcakes with dollops of pink icing. Alicia's eyes sparkled, her nose quivered.

She hopped onto the table and headed for a frothy confection of cherries and marzipan and whipped cream. She stuffed her mouth, three cherries at a time, and though the whipped cream muffled the sound, there was no mistaking her when she yelled,
"I'M BORED!"

Next, it was time for her bath. The Royal Genius Scientist had created a princess-washer just for Alicia. The machine sprinkled the princess with water, then soap. It rinsed her hair until it gleamed. It scrubbed her ears and nose until they were squeaky clean. Alicia couldn't say "I'M BORED." Not because she didn't want to, mind you, but because whenever she opened her mouth, the automatic toothbrush brushed her teeth until they sparkled.

When she was clean, the princess-washer dried her off, slipped a silky nightgown over her head, and popped her onto the conveyor belt that led straight to her bed.

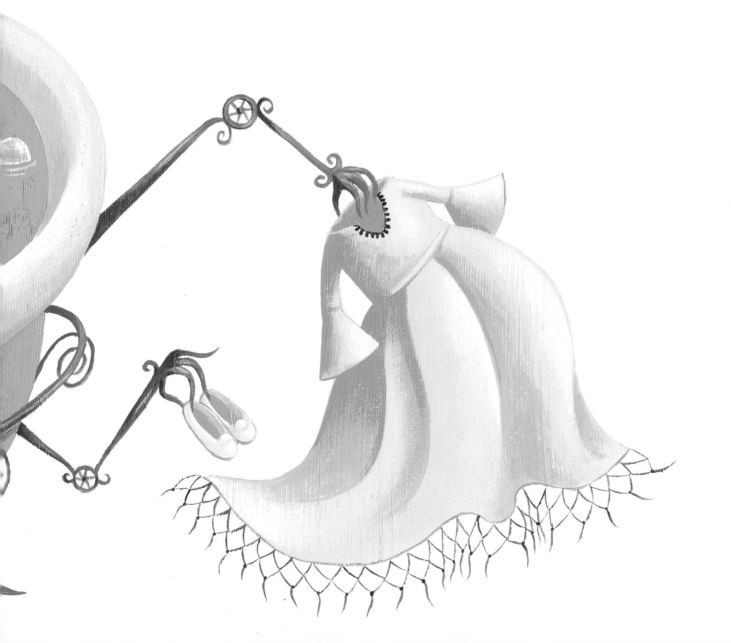

The king was waiting for her, a book on his lap. Alicia snuggled down to listen. It was her favorite, a fine story of knights and ladies and dragons and honor. "Again, again!" she mumbled. She yawned. The king read on until Alicia was asleep.

In all the kingdom, it was the most wonderful moment of the day. Alicia was peaceful. Nobody heard a sound from her. All was calm and serene. Until . . .

Alicia woke up howling. Her cries echoed up and down the hill. The king and queen hurried to her bedside. "Our dear baby, what can we do for you?" asked her anxious father. "Is there anything I can do to make you smile?"

. . . *And keep quiet,* thought the queen, but she said nothing.

Alicia sniffled. A thought occurred to her. "I want a prince."

The next morning, the royal drums rolled *RA-TA-TA-TAM* in the town square. "Hear ye! Hear ye! Noble gentlemen of all the land, the king promises the hand of his daughter, Princess Alicia, in marriage to the man who can keep her from growing bored!"

All that day, princes traveled to the kingdom. They came in every shape and size and character: ne'er-do-wells and ruffians, snooty ones and mousy ones, meek ones, show-offs, and fast-talkers.

Alicia watched them make their way uphill and down dale and, finally, up the highest hill of all to the castle. One by one, the suitors were presented to Alicia. Each tried to amuse her, but before each was through, Alicia was either asleep or grumbling, "I'm bored."

Finally, the last suitor arrived. He was announced as Prince Connor.
Connor had arrived on horseback, a huge cardboard box strapped
to his side. He dismounted and pushed the box toward Alicia.

Alicia had never seen such a warm and friendly smile.
He didn't seem afraid of her at all.

Instead, he tugged the end of the string that tied the box. Alicia was puzzled. The only thing in the box was paper, sheets and sheets of paper. She was gathering herself to yell when the prince seized a large sheet of paper and folded it. He folded it again and again. A fine house appeared in his hands. Alicia was fascinated.

"Why don't you try to make something – it could be anything you want," the prince suggested to her.

Alicia practiced making things from paper. When she got bored with paper, she learned to paint, then to knit, then to hook rugs, and then to grow wheat. She learned to play the horn.

In the years that followed, Princess Alicia and Prince Connor married, and together they built paper castles to delight their children.

They all lived happily until the end of time. Best of all, nobody ever again heard the princess say, "I'M BORED!'